# RACING SHADOWS
## A HIGH SPEED QUEST FOR JUSTICE

CHUCK SUAVE

Also, By Chuck
Short Stories And Tall Tales

# Table of Contents

Visit Chuck Suave at:

www.chucksuave.com[1]

---

# COPYRIGHT NOTICE

# AUTHOR'S NOTES

When I released the first edition, I was sure I was done with it. But stories, like memories, have a way of circling back. This second edition is not just a revision; it's a reunion. Within these pages, you'll find chapters that have been shortened and split, enhancing readability and pacing. Mason's early years and his journey into motor racing have been added, and additional refinements to the narrative have been made by my growing skills and experiences.

I revisited every page with fresh eyes and a slightly more caffeinated heart. Characters now speak louder and silences run deeper.

To those who read, reread, and questioned plot twists, especially my good friend Mary, a massive thank you.

Your feedback and critique shaped this version in ways I could not have imagined. I'd tip my hat to you if only I remembered where it had disappeared to.

This edition is yours as much as mine. Your insights gave me the courage to revise, redraw, and reimagine. Thank you for being part of the story's second life.

Whether you are boarding for the first time or hopping back on, I hope you find something here that stays with you.

With ink-stained gratitude,

Chuck Suave.

# INTRODUCTION

Mason Trevallion's life flashed before his eyes. For a heartbeat, he thought he was done for.

A high-pitched scream tore from the engine. He shut out the crowd's roars and cheers, every muscle loose except for his hands, locked white-knuckled on the wheel. The car lurched, and the safety barrier rushed up at him, growing larger with every frantic heartbeat. He'd been in tight corners before, but never one where the margin between skill and death felt this thin.

Tyres screeched. A flash of white. Metal screamed louder than the crowd. Then silence.

Once a Formula One golden boy, Mason Trevallion had burned through fame and fortune on booze, bets, and bad decisions. Now, against all odds, he wore an FBI badge instead of a racing suit.

His return to the racing world wasn't for glory; it was for answers.

Eva Rossini, his sharp-eyed partner, didn't share his nostalgia for the track. She wanted results, and the Racing Shadows' pit-crew *accidents* were piling up too neatly to be coincidental.

Behind the glamour of high-speed circuits lay something darker: hidden rooms, whispered deals, and shadows moving where the sunlight never touched.

Every lap would draw them closer to the truth, or to the crash waiting at the finish line.

Justice had a price, and Mason was about to find out if he could still afford it.

# CHAPTER ONE

Mason Trevallion leaned against the fence at the Racing Shadows' pit wall. The frantic, choreographed chaos of the pit lane reminded him of his years behind the wheel in Formula One. Engines roared, and the acrid scent of burnt rubber clung to the air.

This was the Las Vegas Grand Prix, and everything in Vegas was bigger, brighter, and bolder. Mason had told himself it was good to be back, but he wasn't here to drive. He was here to hunt.

Inside the pit garage, the banter was raucous, a lively mix of jokes and nerves, but the engine noise drowned it out. Mason crossed to the garage when a flash of movement caught his eye: the petite figure of his new FBI partner.

Eva Rossini dodged and weaved through swarms of mechanics, technicians, reporters, and VIPs. Her gaze darted from one detail to the next as she strode toward Mason. "God, I can't believe this!" she shouted beside him.

He could almost taste the energy. This was what he used to live for: the adrenaline rush, the rhythm of speed.

A series of incidents they were investigating had resulted in serious injury to several pit crew members and damage to expensive equipment. Whispers rippled through the paddock, each more paranoid than the last. Mason and Eva had to move carefully; one wrong question could spook the culprit.

One of the mechanics, injured during a pit stop practice, sat slumped in a folding chair, his arm bound in a splint. Eva approached him.

Mason saw how agitated the man looked as she began asking questions. Sweat gathered along the man's hairline, his eyes flicking between Eva's badge and the open garage door. Eva knelt beside the mechanic. "What happened?" she asked, her voice low but firm.

The mechanic screwed up his face as he recalled the incident.

Cradling his badly broken left arm, he said, "I'm not sure. I was focused on making the tyre change, ready to give 100 per cent to save a few seconds during the pit stop. Just as I turned to put the wheel away, the car suddenly lurched forward and crushed my arm." He continued, "At the debrief, I said I hadn't done anything differently during the pit stop. The driver did mention his car lurched forward for no apparent reason. It was bizarre."

"Did you notice anything unusual? Anything suspicious?" Eva asked, raising her voice just enough to cut through the noise.

"Nothing out of the ordinary," the mechanic said.

One of the other technicians stood up. "Come to think of it, a strange guy came in earlier. He was watching us. I thought I'd seen him before, and when I looked round again, he'd vanished, like he melted into the shadows."

As he spoke, other pit crew members chimed in, their voices layering over the clatter of tools and hiss of compressors. Many of those stories included sightings of the same stranger.

Mason and Eva shared a look. An unspoken acknowledgement that the pattern was too deliberate to ignore.

Mason spoke quietly to Eva. "This stranger is too much of a coincidence."

Eva agreed. "We've either got ourselves a real joker, or something worse," she said. Her expression tightened, mirroring the tension crawling through Mason's gut.

Each new account heightened their suspicions. This wasn't random sabotage, it was methodical, controlled. And that made it dangerous. Mason's stomach churned. Faces of the injured flashed through his mind: hands crushed, bones shattered, careers ended in seconds.

This wasn't just another case. It was payback. Justice for the people who trusted the system and got broken instead. The track day was coming to a close. Mason turned to Eva. "We need to start looking for this mystery man. Something big is going down, and we must get to the bottom of it."

"It's important we keep this crew safe." Her tone was measured, but her jaw was set: she was already forming a plan.

The investigation began with security footage pulled from racetrack cameras. They peered at every frame, eyes stinging from the flicker of footage, searching for the phantom figure described by the pit crew.

Mason's eyes blurred with fatigue as hours of fuzzy footage replayed. He was just about to call it a night when movement caught his attention. He paused the video and pointed at a dark shape hovering near the Racing Shadows garage.

Mason slammed his fist on the desk. "That's our guy! We have to find out who he is."

"This gives us our first solid clue," Eva said. "Let's track him down and see where that takes us."

Mason pointed out that the restricted area was out of bounds for anyone except authorised personnel, so the mystery man must have had help from inside the team.

The priority was to identify that person. The race against time had just begun, and the stakes were rising.

They began scrutinising the staff documents of the Racing Shadows team, narrowing suspects by height, build, and security access.

Their search turned into a maze of false leads and dead ends, but they persisted, working well into the early hours.

The following morning, they questioned everyone connected with Racing Shadows, from mechanics to team managers. Every question looped back to the same blank space, the stranger without a name.

They discovered new information about what had happened earlier, but it only deepened the mystery.

During a tense discussion with one of the public relations staff, Mason caught an important lead.

Rumours surfaced about the team principal, Lucas Devereaux. It was speculated that Devereaux ruled with manipulation and menace, cutting down anyone who challenged his authority.

The puzzle was taking shape as more pieces fell into place. Mason and Eva knew they still had a long way to go. It wouldn't be easy catching whoever orchestrated this, but neither of them knew how to quit.

They both shut down their computers and tidied away the documents on the desk. Their journey had only just begun, but now it had momentum. A purpose. A pulse.

To protect the innocent and expose the truth.

Mason woke up groggy from a poor night's sleep. Dreams of the pit lane, screams, crashes, faces, still clung to him like smoke.

In the office, he met Eva, who seemed sharp, composed, and frustratingly energetic.

They sat across the desk from each other. The room was dimly lit, files and evidence strewn across every surface.

The mountain of paperwork seemed to lean towards them, a silent reminder of how little progress they'd made.

"What if this is more than just targeting the pit crew?" Eva asked, flipping through another personnel file.

"What do you mean?" Mason replied, rubbing his eyes.

"I've been going through the team's personnel files. There's a pattern emerging." She paused. "Each incident involved someone who had just discovered some sort of wrongdoing within the racing team."

Her notes were underlined with red ink; arrows, names and dates, all pointing to corruption, blackmail, and internal power plays.

Mason had a feeling this wasn't good. If Eva was right, someone inside Racing Shadows was cleaning house, silencing anyone who got too close to the truth.

"This isn't about nicking stuff," Mason said. "It's about control, covering dirty deals, shutting people up before they talk."

"Exactly," Eva said. She rubbed her temples as the same names circled back, contracts rewritten, bonuses erased, silence bought.

Mason's pen hovered above a photo. 'They're cleaning house,' he muttered." Suddenly, his phone buzzed against the table, breaking the quiet.

The screen glowed with an anonymous number.

***There's a hidden room in the team garage.***

***You need to find it and see what's inside.***

Eva read the text over his shoulder, her eyes widening. "What are we going to do about that?" she asked.

"You stay here and look for more evidence," Mason replied. "I'll check this out."

# CHAPTER TWO

The tip-off led Mason through a maze of dimly lit service corridors beneath the stands. The roar of the racetrack above echoed overhead like distant thunder.

He stopped before a heavy metal door marked *'AUTHORISED PERSONNEL ONLY'.*

He tried the handle, but it was locked. Mason crouched, pulled a thin tool from his jacket, and worked it into the mechanism. A soft click rewarded him. He eased the door open and stepped inside. The room was dark and stale, heavy with dust and machine oil.

Papers littered desks. Photographs, news cuttings, and pit reports were taped haphazardly across the walls, a timeline of disasters.

As Mason scanned the room, he realised it was more than a storage space; it was a shrine to sabotage.

A shiver traced his spine as anticipation mixed with unease.

He moved closer to study the images. Each showed accidents, damage, and headlines about "unexplained" mechanical failures.

His mind filled with questions. Who collected all this? Why hide it here? Was this the work of the mysterious figure, or someone even closer to home?

Mason didn't hear a thing until he did: a faint click of a door handle and someone stepping into the room. Instinct hit him hard; every nerve lit up. He spun around, heart hammering.

A figure stood in the gloom.

The stranger's silhouette was carved from the single beam of light from the roof vent; still, deliberate.

Of course, it was impossible to know what this stranger wanted, but Mason didn't need to guess. Every instinct screamed danger.

This one wasn't here to talk. His fight-or-flight instinct took over. He had been in mortal peril before and was no stranger to combat. He stepped forward.

His focus narrowed on the stranger's stance, weight, balance and economy of motion. All tells of a trained fighter. Ready for any confrontation, he forced down his fear. The stranger tilted his head, sneering, then lunged. Mason launched into action. Training took over; Krav Maga drills burned into muscle memory. His strike aimed for the solar plexus, but the stranger slipped aside, too fast.

Mason's punches and kicks met air, while his opponent landed blow after blow with brutal precision. The stranger was anticipating every move, dancing around Mason, each strike colder, more calculated.

He delivered a double-fisted blow to Mason's chest, then a roundhouse kick that spun him sideways.

Mason fought back with all his might but felt the tide shift. The fight had become one-sided, and he was the prey.

The stranger moved with unnatural precision, raining rapid combinations of punches and kicks. A spinning backhand connected squarely with Mason's temple, sending a shockwave through his skull, followed by a knife-hand strike to his neck. Pain flared white-hot.

His opponent was formidable and well-trained. Mason reeled, his vision flashing with every hit. He tasted blood and adrenaline.

He was in big trouble.

Eva burst into the room, drawn by the sounds of impact and the crash of furniture.

She was skilled in unarmed combat and didn't hesitate. "Get back from him!" she shouted, launching a front kick followed by an elbow strike.

Her blows sliced through the air but met only the stranger's shifting silhouette. He wheeled behind her, a blur of movement, and countered with a spinning kick that narrowly missed her head.

Eva blocked with her upper arm. The impact numbed it instantly. She hissed in pain but held her stance.

The rain of blows to her arms, head, and torso made recovery nearly impossible. She covered her face and ribs, fending off attacks that came too fast to read.

Mason lay battered on the floor, vision swimming, unable to rise. Eva tried to fight back, but the stranger proved too good. Every move she made, he was already there.

A sharp elbow caught her jaw, and stars exploded behind her eyes. Her body went slack.

Then, the stranger stopped.

He looked down at Eva and Mason, both sprawled on the floor, their breaths ragged, their bodies bruised and broken by the fight.

He laughed, a low, cold sound, then turned and walked calmly out of the room, leaving only silence in his wake.

The only sounds in the room came from their laboured breathing. As the adrenaline ebbed, Mason's thoughts began to race. Who was that man? How did he know about the hidden room? Was he part of Devereaux's web, or something larger?

His attention shifted to Eva. He crawled towards her, pain flaring through his ribs, and gently cradled her head. "Eva! Are you okay?" he asked, his voice hoarse.

Eva groaned and forced herself upright, wincing. She rubbed her arms. "I'm all right," she said, "Just a few bruises and tons of pain everywhere. Nothing I can't handle, though."

Mason exhaled, relief and anger mixing in his chest. "That was close," he said. "If you hadn't shown up, I'd be a smear on the floor."

Eva managed a weak smile. "We make a good team," she said. "Even when we get flattened."

Mason glanced toward the open door, where the corridor light bled across the floor. "He let us live," he said quietly. "Why?"

Eva followed his gaze. "Maybe to send a message."

They sat in silence for a moment, the hum of the racetrack faint above them. Mason's pulse slowed, but the knot in his stomach remained. Somewhere beyond that door, the truth was still hiding, bigger and darker than either of them had imagined.

Eva pushed herself to her feet and offered him a hand. "We're not finished," she said. "Whoever that was, he's part of the bigger picture, and we're going to find out what."

Mason took her hand, pulling himself upright with a grimace. "Then let's start with this room," he said, scanning the scattered photos and files. "If he came here to protect something, it's in these walls."

Eva nodded, stepping closer to the wall of evidence. Her fingers hovered over a photograph of Lucas Devereaux shaking hands with a man in a dark suit. The man's face was blurred, but the silhouette looked hauntingly familiar.

Mason's voice was low, almost to himself. "Every race has a finish line, but we're only on the first lap."

# CHAPTER THREE

Mexico is the next venue on the Formula One calendar.

Bright red and green Mexican flags snapped in the wind above the grandstands, casting jagged shadows across the Formula One logo.

Arriving at the racetrack, Mason and Eva wove through the throng of spectators, heading straight for the Racing Shadows garage, senses buzzing with the hum of engines and the scent of sizzling street food.

Spectators packed the grandstands on both sides, their excited chatter and chants swelling as Free Practice 1 approached.

The aroma of spicy tacos and savoury empanadas drifted from nearby food trucks, mingling with the tang of tequila in margaritas.

Palm trees and towering cacti shimmered in the searing desert heat, and mirages wavered on the horizon.

Mason and Eva threaded between the bright red Ferraris, sleek silver Mercedes, and vibrant orange McLarens, their polished bodies gleaming under the relentless sun.

Familiar adrenaline prickled Mason's skin, memories of near victories and crushing defeats echoing in his mind as though he were on the track once more.

They ducked into a quieter corner of the garage, muffled from the roar of engines and the clanging of tools echoing around them. Huddled around a worn table, his focus fracturing as familiar garage sounds tugged at memories he had tried to bury.

He tried to concentrate on the task at hand and picked up a diagram of the racetrack. Mason gripped the racetrack diagram, tracing every curve and straight with his finger, just as he had done before races long past.

A nervous rhythm tapped against the paper, betraying his unease. Eva prowled the garage, scanning each mechanic with sharp, calculating eyes. She picked up a spanner from a spotless workbench, surprised by the gleam under the overhead lights. The tools weren't the grimy coated implements she'd expected.

Time was slipping through their fingers; failure wasn't an option if they wanted to protect the drivers. "Time's short," she snapped, scanning the room. "We need to uncover who's behind these accidents." Pressure bore down on them, the distant roar of engines a constant reminder of what was at stake.

Mason's phone buzzed. He frowned at the anonymous message blinking on the screen:

"An accident will unfold during the next race," he read aloud, voice tight with unease. "We have to be ready," he said. "There's no time to lose."

"The next race is only hours away," Eva said. "We have to protect our drivers and unmask whoever is behind this. Before they strike again."

Eva's hand froze over the spanner. Something glinted near the bench, almost invisible, a tiny lens peeking from the shadows. A hidden camera.

"They're watching us," she whispered, barely audible above the engine's roar. Shock jolted through Mason; had someone been tracking their every move?

Eva snatched the camera silently, sliding it into her pocket before anyone noticed. Their fragile rapport with the team couldn't afford a setback like this.

The team's close-knit dynamics meant outsiders were unwelcome. Mason knew resentment could derail the investigation before it even began; they needed the crew on their side.

Doubt crept in, clawing at Mason. Memories surged: nights blurred by binge drinking, debts piled high from gambling and drugs, friends and colleagues walking away, and the ultimate blow, being expelled from Formula One. Each echo threatened to undo him again.

Amid the chaos, Mason's anchor had always been Carlos Morales, best friend and mentor. Carlos's steady voice reminded him to trust his instincts, to lean on those who truly had his back.

Mason inhaled sharply, forcing the lingering self-doubt away. Focus sharpened; this case wasn't just another investigation. It was his chance to prove he could still get things right.

Mason's phone vibrated again, jolting him. Another anonymous message flashed on the screen:

***Two high-profile individuals are holding a secret meeting.***

Eva's eyes narrowed at the screen. They would have to infiltrate this meeting.

Mason typed a cautious reply: ***Need more information.***

He didn't expect a reply. Moments later, the phone buzzed again. No text, just a photograph. Mason's eyes widened as he swiped it open.

The image revealed Lucas Devereaux, their team principal, in a heated argument with Olivia Dupont, a journalist with murky ties to organised crime.

He thrust the phone towards Eva. "Olivia's tangled in this as well. We need to figure out their involvement." They needed answers.

Hatching a high-risk plan, Mason and Eva knew there was no room for hesitation.

They left the garage, each step echoing the tension in their chests as they approached Lucas's office.

Mason gave Eva a nod. She inhaled sharply, pushed the door open, and stepped inside, Mason close behind.

Crossing the threshold, both felt the gravity of their decision; there was no turning back.

Power, manipulation, and hidden agendas waited inside; one wrong move could undo everything.

Lucas looked up, eyebrows drawn. "What do you want?" His voice was low, edged with arrogance.

"We know what you're planning," Mason said, heart hammering. "We know about the sabotage ... and your involvement."

Lucas's laugh was sharp and dismissive. "You've no proof? You're grasping at straws."

Mason's gaze flicked to Olivia. She stood unmoving behind Lucas, a hand resting lightly on his shoulder, expression unreadable.

"We have proof linking you both," Eva interjected, voice steady.

Olivia's face remained a mask, radiating authority, as if she already held every answer.

"You think you can take us down?" Lucas sneered at Eva. "Ants trying to topple giants."

Mason didn't flinch. "We're not intimidated. The truth will surface, and we will bring you down."

Silence stretched, thick and heavy, as Mason and Eva met the cold eyes of Lucas and Olivia. The danger was palpable, but they were ready.

Olivia's voice cut through the tension, calm yet unnerving. "You think you know everything," she said, eyes locked on Mason. "There's always more than meets the eye."

Lucas leapt to his feet, face flushed with rage. "Get out!" he spat, jabbing toward the door. "Now! Or you'll regret crossing me."

Recognising they had rattled Lucas and Olivia and glimpsed the edge of a larger conspiracy, they backed out. They needed to regroup, gather more evidence, and return stronger.

# CHAPTER FOUR

Back in the garage, they spread the evidence across the workbench, each document and photo forming a piece of the puzzle.

Eva's hand froze over a folder. "We have a mole," she whispered, her eyes widening. "All the evidence points to one person."

"Not a word to anyone yet," Mason cautioned.

Revealing the mole too soon could shatter trust within the team. Mason and Eva needed to verify every detail before acting.

The hunt for the traitor was urgent. How much had they leaked? Who was pulling the strings? Mason's mind raced through possible precautions.

Mason and Eva would confront the mole at once.

Alex, the mole, was hunched over an engine in the corner. Mason and Eva approached from opposite sides, boxing him in without alerting the others.

"You've been playing a dangerous game," Mason hissed, keeping his voice low enough to avoid prying ears.

Alex lifted his head, eyes defiant. "I don't know what you mean. You've got nothing on me!"

He planted his hands on the engine, jaw tight, refusing to yield to intimidation.

Eva stepped closer. "We've got plenty." She flipped open the folder, each piece of evidence a bullet aimed straight at him.

"Every breadcrumb leads back here," Mason said. "It's time you answered for your actions."

Alex's defiance flickered. "You think threats will make me break? I'm not afraid."

"Fear has a way of showing up," Eva pressed. "Maybe you should be more afraid than you think."

Questions came in rapid succession; neither Mason nor Eva relented.

"We have evidence tying you to the attacks," Mason stated, his voice low and firm.

Eva stepped in. "Your alibi doesn't hold. You claimed to be in the garage every time, but witnesses place you outside, moments before each incident."

They moved in a practised rhythm: Mason opening, Eva following up, a choreography of interrogation.

Eva slammed the folder onto the car beside Alex. "We know what you've done and how you've manipulated the team. Now tell us why. We need the truth!"

Alex's confident mask cracked for a heartbeat. Uncertainty flickered across his face; he wasn't walking away this time.

"Why does anyone act?" Alex spat, his voice rough. "Power, money, control. It's dog-eat-dog, Trevallion, you should know that."

"We're not playing games! We want answers and justice!" Eva's voice rose, catching the attention of mechanics nearby.

Alex let out a bitter laugh. "Justice? Funny word. You can't change a thing, you're pawns in a much bigger game."

"Maybe we are pawns," Mason said, stepping back to give Alex room. "But even pawns can take kings down."

Evidence alone wouldn't be enough to break him. They needed leverage, something that spoke to his conscience.

Mason gestured subtly to the watching mechanics. "These people trust you. Can you keep betraying that trust?"

Alex's gaze flicked to his colleagues, then back to Mason. Doubt crept in, slow but undeniable.

"What do you want from me?" he asked, his voice quieter now.

"We want the truth," Eva said softly as she stepped closer. "We need to know who's behind the attacks, and why you're protecting them."

Alex hesitated, caught in a moment of clarity. There was no escape; he could only confess to lift the burden of his secret.

"I didn't want to be involved," Alex admitted, his voice trembling, "They threatened my family. I had to cooperate, or they'd be hurt."

Mason and Eva exchanged a silent acknowledgement. Alex had been coerced, dragged into betrayal to protect his family, a revelation that shifted everything.

Finally, Alex slumped. "I'll do whatever it takes. I'll tell you everything," he sighed. "But you must promise to protect me and my family. They're the reason I was forced into this."

Mason extended a reassuring hand. "We'll place you and your family in protective custody until you testify, and beyond if necessary. You needn't fear anymore."

Mason and Eva knew they needed allies within the pit crew. someone capable of standing up to the saboteurs from the inside.

Eva scanned the team in her mind, weighing skills, loyalty, and character. There had to be one person who craved the truth as much as they did. Someone they could trust to unravel the sabotage.

Her choice fell on Jack Thompson, a brilliant, sharp-witted mechanic. A loner since joining the team, he had never fully fit in. His unconventional skills were risky, but his results were undeniable.

Mason nodded. Jack was perfect. He would let Eva handle the delicate task of winning Jack's trust.

Jack hunched over an engine, grease staining his hands. Eva approached, calm but firm. "Jack, we need your help."

He looked up, his grin curling. "What's in it for me?"

Eva studied him, trying to read the expression behind the grin. Nothing. He was an enigma.

It was clear: Jack played by his own rules. For the team's safety, they had to appeal to his pride and leverage his exceptional skill.

"We want to stop the accidents," Eva said, leaning slightly forward. "You don't play by the rules, you take risks, and that's exactly why we need you."

Jack's eyebrows shot up, eyes glinting. Eva could tell he couldn't resist; the recognition of his skills as the team's best mechanic was exactly the lure he needed.

"All right, you've got me," Jack said, a smirk tugging at his lips. "I'm in."

Eva exhaled, relieved. They now had a formidable ally in Jack.

With Jack on their side, their odds of stopping the saboteurs and protecting the team had just improved dramatically.

With their strategy set, Mason, Eva and Jack set off towards Olivia's office, tension tightening with every step, unaware of what traps awaited.

Mason's hand gripped the handle. He pushed it open and strode inside.

Olivia looked up from her papers, eyes narrowing as Mason entered.

Jack followed, standing beside Mason, while Eva leaned against the wall to his left. They projected a quiet, formidable presence.

"I expected you," Olivia said, eyes flicking from Mason to Eva, then Jack.

Mason met her gaze steadily. "We know you're involved. There's nowhere left to hide."

A smirk tugged at Olivia's lips. "And why do you think that?"

Eva stepped forward, tossing the evidence onto Olivia's desk. Papers rattled. "We have proof linking you to Lucas Devereaux. You said knowledge is power, we finally understand what you meant."

Olivia flinched at the sudden movement but quickly regained composure, leaning over the desk to examine the contents.

"Impressive," Olivia said, smoothly, "but what will exposing me achieve? The truth won't save anyone; it will only bring chaos."

Mason didn't flinch. They had the truth, and no smooth words would make him waver.

"We pursue truth and justice," Mason said firmly. "We won't let corruption or lies reign, here or anywhere."

Olivia held Mason's gaze a beat longer, then rose slowly, voice low and threatening. A chill ran down the trio's spines.

"You're sharper than I expected," she said, locking eyes with Mason. "But beware, the truth reveals more than you anticipate."

Silence stretched across the room. Olivia's words hinted at depths yet to be revealed. The investigation was far from over; this was merely a glimpse.

Olivia sank back into her chair, weighing how much to reveal. She recognised the trio as formidable adversaries.

"You think you know everything," she murmured. "Some secrets are buried so deep they may never see daylight."

Mason stared at her. "We'll uncover those secrets, no matter the cost. You may hold the cards, but we have aces up our sleeves." With that, the trio turned and left.

Questions churned in Mason's mind. What would come next?

The encounter had only strengthened his resolve. He would press on, unearthing the truth and holding the culprits to account.

# CHAPTER FIVE

Arriving at Racing Shadows headquarters, Eva muttered to Mason, "We're entering the lion's den. Let's hope our luck holds, like Daniel's."

The glass doors slid open, and they scanned the foyer for the reception desk. They gave their names, clipped on their security passes, and headed for the lifts.

Mason nodded. "We have to be very careful. We can't afford even a single mistake."

Mason pressed the button and glanced up when the doors opened. Three mirrored walls reflected the tension etched across their faces.

The doors closed behind them. Mason and Eva stood in silence, each calculating their next move.

Eva focused on the illuminated numbers climbing to the middle floors. "We can't underestimate anyone," she muttered.

The tenth floor lit up, and the doors parted, revealing a bustling corridor filled with people engaged in various activities.

Eva and Mason moved through the crowd, whispers trailing behind them as they passed workstations and conference rooms.

Mason kept silent, guarding Alex's identity. He had promised Alex safety until the investigation was over.

Room 1020 was their base of operations. Once inside, Eva said, "People are already speculating about the mole," as she laid out pictures and documents on the table.

"Let's get started and review what we have so far," Mason replied. Eva continued to organise the evidence they'd compiled.

They began reviewing their findings. They needed to ensure their evidence was airtight; otherwise, the conspirators would exploit any weaknesses.

They discussed their next move, and an uneasy feeling tugged at the back of their minds. With each step forward into dangerous territory, they would be risking an awful lot. The investigation needed to progress, and they were prepared to dive headlong into whatever came next. At this point, they were all in.

Mason sat, tapping his fingers against the table. His focus was on the evidence before him.

However, he knew he could rely on Eva. As the lead investigator, however, the burden and responsibility rested squarely on his shoulders.

Eva recognised the signs in Mason and shared his concerns. "We can't lose hope now. We knew this was going to be a difficult road. I'm here every step of the way."

"I can't help but suspect everybody's intentions. How can we trust anyone when we don't know who's on our side?" he told her.

"Trust is such a fragile thing. We can only go forward, keeping our cards close." She turned an old photograph in her hands, then set it down.

"But we need to find others to help us, those who know something is going on, have scruples and will fight with us." Mason sighed.

Eva smiled a little. "There are people who want to find the truth, like us. We just need to find them."

Mason felt better after this pep talk with Eva. He sat up, thought for a moment, and said, "Let's contact the team individually and in secret. Find out what everyone's views are on the investigation and establish some level of trust. If we can all work together, we have a fighting chance of uncovering the truth."

They wrote down each team member's name and how best to approach them. They would have to be very careful. They didn't want any hint that Alex was helping their cause. They had to protect him at all costs.

Trying to establish who they could trust would not be easy. Betrayal could come from anyone, and danger was everywhere.

"We're not backing down," Mason said firmly. We're the FBI. That's not our way."

Eva reassured him with a firm grip on his arm.

They knew they simply couldn't ignore what was happening now. They had achieved so much that backing down wasn't an option.

They nodded to each other, gathered their gear, and stepped out of the meeting room.

The time to act was now. They must find out who would be loyal and who would betray them. They had made promises. All those who suffered at the hands of greedy saboteurs would be brought to justice.

Mason and Eva took the lift to ground level and left the office complex. They knew what they had to do and how they would achieve it.

They headed back to Racing Shadows' garage for the next step in the investigation. The team, once close, was becoming fractured by distrust and secrecy. Mason looked around the room for friendly faces, trying to determine who he could trust.

He looked across at Olivia as she passed the garage. He still felt uneasy about what she knew. Olivia was difficult to read, which worried him. He had always been a good judge of character, but with her, he couldn't tell.

Eva had been watching Mason for days and realised he was struggling. She called Carlos Morales, whom she believed could help Mason regain his focus.

She wasn't sure how Mason would react, but despite her reservations, she needed Carlos's help now more than ever.

She picked up her phone and dialled his number. "Carlos, it's Eva. I'm worried about Mason and need your help. Yes, the doubts are back. Could you give him one of your famous pep talks?"

"Yes, Eva, that's OK. I can meet you tomorrow night. How does 8:00 pm sound? Where will you be?"

"We can meet at a restaurant nearby. I'll book a table and send you the address. Oh, we have identified the mole," she continued. "No one can find out just yet. We need to proceed very cautiously. I'll explain more when we see you tomorrow."

"I'll bring along a friend too. She'll be very interested in your investigation."

Eva had suggested to Mason that they go out for dinner to take a break from the investigation. She wasn't sure how Mason would react to her calling Carlos. Mason and Eva were at the table when Carlos arrived at the restaurant. He was a fine figure of a man despite his age.

He hugged Mason tightly and lifted Eva's hand, kissing it like a true gentleman.

Turning around, he introduced his companion, Natalie Lindberg, a journalist and a long-time friend. When he contacted her about the investigation, she was eager to be part of the team. The bonus would be exposing influential and corrupt individuals.

Natalie explained that she and Carlos went way back to the days before he became a racing engineer, and, with a woman's intuition, Eva guessed they had been more than just friends.

Natalie offered her connections and knowledge within the media industry. She assured Mason that she would spread the findings of his investigation using all her media contacts and social platforms. She despised entitled people who preyed on weaker individuals.

The different skill sets their new allies brought convinced Mason they could blow this conspiracy apart.

The harder they worked, gathering information and fitting the pieces together, the more complications they encountered. The forces fighting them continued to keep them from completing their investigation.

The risks were high, but so were the rewards. They'd known from the start that this was about more than pit crew accidents.

They were pleasantly surprised by how many pledged allegiance to them in some form or another. They continued to follow through on the plan to speak secretly with individual team members.

Natalie suggested she could leak small snippets of information to stir up public interest. The allegations of corruption and deceit would spread quickly through the public domain, and public interest would surge.

The fallout from the leaked information put Mason and his team under intense scrutiny from the public and the FBI. But no matter how difficult the obstacles, they would ensure the truth would come out.

# CHAPTER SIX

Eva knew little about Mason's past and felt honoured that he was opening up to her. He carried the weight of his past mistakes like ballast, dragging behind him.

He spoke of his days as a Formula One driver during his debut season. Everything felt heady and exhilarating, with zealous fans surrounding him everywhere he went. There was too much money, more than a young man like him could handle. Back then, he was always in clubs and casinos with a glamorous model on his arm, and rarely without a drink in his hand.

The Playboy lifestyle, he admitted, had been his undoing. The gambling habit escalated. He lost far more than he won, which, in turn, fuelled his descent into alcohol.

At that time, friends like Carlos tried to make him see where he was heading. Young, arrogant, and convinced that he could handle it all.

Carlos, who had been his race engineer, tried to steer Mason back onto the straight and narrow, but it was too late; Mason had already broken too many rules.

His contract was terminated halfway through the season, and he was thrown out of Formula One.

Had it not been for Carlos, he wasn't sure how things would have turned out. Carlos pulled him back from the brink, mentoring and coaching him through those difficult times.

Thanks to Carlos's influence, Mason turned his life around and eventually joined the FBI. He owed Carlos a huge debt of gratitude.

Eva listened, aware of the weight he carried on his shoulders. "You are not alone in this," she assured him. "I am with you until the end."

"Thank you for not judging me," he said. Their eyes met; an intimacy lingered between them, a 'will they, won't they' moment. However, they both understood that it would have been madness to pursue anything romantic just now.

They were about to face their greatest challenge and could not afford to jeopardise it.

This investigation would determine both their fates. They would prevail; there was no other option.

Now, with allies by their side, they would unite and be ready for whatever challenges lay ahead.

Mason set off to find Jack and update him on the progress of the investigation. He found him repairing an engine and went over to him.

"Jack," Mason said to catch his attention. "Alex is the mole, but you must keep this to yourself. He's under protective custody. We want you to stay alert around the garage. Keep gathering evidence and report on any rumours circulating. If anything comes up about Alex, let me know as soon as possible."

"You can count on me, mate," he said. "Nobody suspects the mechanic who's always up to his elbows in grease." Mason nodded in appreciation.

Just then, a voice sent shivers down Mason's spine. Olivia Dupont was approaching him with a sinister grin.

"Mason," Olivia said coolly. "I heard you've been digging for more evidence and uncovered more secrets. What a fascinating turn of events." Mason sensed there was more behind her words than she was letting on.

"There's a lot more going on than you're aware of," Mason replied. "You should watch your back, Olivia."

Olivia smirked. "I always do," she said as she turned on her heels and strode out through the garage.

As she left, a thought struck Mason. She had her share of secrets and was overly confident she wouldn't be caught. He suspected she was holding something over someone, leverage she could wield when the time came.

Mason needed to update Eva on his encounter with Olivia. They retreated to a corner of the garage, away from prying eyes.

"We have people on the inside now," Eva said. "They want to end this corruption as much as we do."

Mason crossed his arms and leaned back on a nearby tool cart. "We're approaching a pivotal moment in the investigation, so we need to be more vigilant than ever," he said firmly.

"The first thing we need to do is get another base of operations," said Eva. "I feel someone is out there watching us."

"I'll call Carlos," Mason replied. "He's got contacts who will secure us a new place."

Carlos had come through for them. He secured a suite of offices large enough to house Mason and his team.

Mason and Eva spent long hours there, running on adrenaline. They needed to ensure their evidence was solid and untainted by anything that Alex might have leaked.

Various documents and photographs lay sprawled across the desks.

Eva pointed to a series of photographs. "There's a pattern here. Each incident implicates a separate member of the pit crew."

Mason looked over.

"There's a common denominator too," she continued. "They all have a history with Lucas Devereaux. This could be the evidence we need to put him away."

"It seems he has his skeletons in the closet," she added. "We need to expose Devereaux as the puppet master before he can strike again."

Mason jumped from his chair, exclaiming, "We'll gather the evidence we have against Devereaux and shatter his illusion completely. The world needs to know about his involvement in these acts of sabotage."

They knew how dangerous Devereaux could be, but they were committed to seeking justice. Every instinct screamed at Mason not to let Devereaux escape; the closer they got, the more ruthless he would become.

Eva clapped him on the shoulder and said softly, "We're almost there. We'll close the net on Devereaux and his cronies, but we must remain vigilant when confronting him."

Mason agreed. After a gruelling day, he closed his laptop and secured the evidence in the safe. He knew revealing the truth would come at a cost.

Mason would convince his allies that the evidence was compelling against the perpetrators. Their confidence in taking on the individuals behind the sabotage grew with each new piece of proof.

# CHAPTER SEVEN

Back in the office, an envelope awaited them. One of the main sponsors of Racing Shadows, Tommy Westwood, was hosting a party at his mansion. Mason and Eva were on the guest list.

They had seen his name several times during the investigation. He was on the list of primary suspects.

"That's weird!" Eva said. "Either it's a coincidence or he's onto us and this is a fishing expedition."

Mason's phone rang; it was Carlos. Natalie had uncovered financial documents linking Lucas to Tommy and organised crime syndicates. Mason and Eva would use this information to corner Tommy into revealing any connection to Devereaux.

On the night of the party, Mason wore a black tuxedo and bow tie, while Eva looked stunning in a silver dress that hugged her curves. They stood on the lawn, transfixed by the magnificent mansion. Music and laughter spilled from the house as guests drifted between the gardens and ballroom.

"We can't afford any mistakes tonight," said Mason.

Eva nodded. "No slip-ups. We can't blow our investigation."

As they entered the grand hall, eyes turned in their direction. Mason knew it wasn't him they noticed; it was Eva, radiant in her dress. The room shimmered with wealth; tuxedos, bow ties, and gowns glittering with jewels brighter than the chandeliers. Tipsy gossip mingled with clinking glasses as a string quartet played in front of a bay window.

They spotted Tommy Westwood. He stood in the centre, holding court, speaking loudly to impress the crowd that fawned over his every word.

Mason couldn't help but stare.

Eva whispered, "You'll give the game away if you keep staring. We need to get close without raising suspicion."

"Let's separate and mingle," he suggested. "Be careful and observant. Someone must know something about Westwood."

Mason and Eva split up and blended into the glittering crowd, making small talk as they hunted for clues.

Mason approached a group of men, captivated by a pompous man retelling an account of a yacht race. The conversation soon dwindled into idle chatter about money, holidays and egos.

Time to provoke a reaction, Mason thought. He targeted the mouthpiece. "It's uncanny how orchestrated these events seem." He raised an eyebrow, gauging interest. "The media is full of theories. Have you heard any rumours about who might be involved?"

One man hesitated, looked around, then admitted, "There are rumours... of corruption and deceit running deep in the industry."

Mason caught his breath. "What do you mean?" he whispered, feigning interest.

The man looked even more cautiously around. "I've heard rumours of dodgy business dealings and some unknown assailant. No names yet, though."

Eva had similar encounters. A tipsy lady revealed gossip about gangsters' involvement, slurring slightly, before begging Eva to keep her name out of it.

Mason and Eva caught each other's eye across the room, regrouping briefly to compare notes before making their move towards Westwood and his entourage.

Mason arrived first and stood on the edge of the group. Eva took the right. Their cover identities: an ambitious driver and a respected journalist.

Later, Mason and Westwood's eyes met fleetingly. Mason caught a flicker of recognition, or suspicion, before Westwood turned to another guest.

He knew he had to tread carefully; this could be the breakthrough they sought.

"It's chilling how these incidents have affected so many lives," Eva remarked, steering the discussion with measured precision.

Tommy laughed, launching a well-rehearsed speech about company safety protocols and rigorous training, deflecting attention from the accidents.

"Are you a bit defensive there, Tommy?" Mason probed.

"What about enquiries into these accidents?" Eva pressed, observing every micro-expression.

Westwood faltered briefly. "We take these incidents seriously," he said smoothly. "Everything is being investigated correctly."

Mason sensed an opportunity. He leaned closer, lowering his voice. "Rumours suggest these accidents aren't coincidences."

"Rumours are idle gossip," Westwood countered, unease creeping into his posture.

"These events are too well-coordinated to be random. I hear someone is blowing the whistle," Eva pressed. "The FBI is involved," she added, letting the challenge hang in the air.

Westwood's composure cracked, and he forced a laugh, changing the subject. "I hope they get the answers they want. There's nothing true about these absurd rumours."

Mason's frustration grew; the truth about Westwood remained just out of reach.

Then he dropped his bombshell: Natalie's financial evidence. "What about the shenanigans at Racing Shadows? The links to organised crime?"

The room fell silent. All eyes were on them, curiosity and apprehension mingling.

"Now, will you tell us the truth?" Mason demanded. "Or shall I reveal more damning evidence?"

Westwood's composure was shattered. Anger and desperation flared; he darted toward the exit.

Mason acted instantly, diving forward to handcuff him.

Chaos erupted. Guests scrambled, some intervening, others retreating. Eva joined Mason, helping restrain Westwood until the authorities arrived.

As the police led him away, Mason shared a triumphant smile with Eva. A key player behind the sabotage was finally facing justice.

A commotion at the entrance drew their attention. They arrived to see Natalie Lindburg arguing with one of Westwood's henchmen.

"You can't keep hiding the truth!" her voice echoing through the hall.

"Truth is subjective," the henchman mocked.

Mason stepped forward. "What's happening here? Let go of her!"

The henchman released Natalie. Relieved, she explained, "He tried to silence me to stop me revealing Westwood's deeds."

Outnumbered, the henchman shrugged and retreated, leaving Mason, Eva, and Natalie alone.

Natalie grinned wryly. "Carlos told me everything; I'm no stranger to events like this."

"We need all the friends we can get," Eva said warmly.

Mason looked at both women. "There's still work to do, but we can crack this investigation."

Eva nodded. "We won't rest until all perpetrators are brought down."

They left the mansion, arm in arm.

Back at the office, Mason and Eva reviewed the past few days. They were closing in on the remaining conspirators. Mason saw the effect of the investigation on everyone but wouldn't let it crush morale.

"Now that we know about Westwood and have Alex's testimony, we have enough to nail Devereaux," Mason said. "We need to catch him off guard."

Eva nodded slowly. "We must stay one step ahead. If he gets wind of how much we know, everything could blow up."

"I have an idea. We need to infiltrate his inner circle to gather the final pieces before taking him down," Mason said, leaning back with a smile.

"How?" Eva asked. "It won't be easy to convince someone to turn against Devereaux."

"We need someone from the inside," Mason answered. "Someone close to him."

"Who?" Eva pressed.

Inspiration struck her. "Maria Sanchez. She's been his right-hand woman for years and knows his operations intimately."

Mason paused. "Maria is fiercely loyal. She won't betray him lightly."

"We must earn her trust. If she believes we have everyone's best interests at heart, she might help."

Mason understood the risk but felt excitement at outwitting Devereaux.

"Alright. Let's reach out to Maria. Time to move this investigation forward."

Eva's mind raced. "Carlos has contacts in the racing world. He can approach Maria and see if she's open to talking."

"I'll contact him. This is right up the sly old fox's street," Mason chuckled.

"If she agrees, he can arrange a meeting. Then it's up to us to convince her."

Mason winked. "You can be quite devious."

"If this works, and Maria becomes our ally, that might tip the balance in our favour and uncover evidence against others," Eva said.

Carlos worked his magic. Maria agreed to hear them out, hinting she sometimes disagreed with Devereaux's methods.

The meeting was arranged.

"I knew you'd eventually come knocking at my door. I just didn't think it would be to recruit me to your side."

"What do you mean?" Eva asked.

"Who do you think has been sending the anonymous texts? When I learned about Devereaux's link to Westwood, that was the last straw. I got in touch to guide the investigation, without revealing myself."

Meetings with Maria had to be held oi secret. They would meet in late-night coffee shops or have whispered phone calls.

Maria revealed information she'd found in a journal, hidden in a shoebox. It detailed connections to Olivia Dupont and Westwood, links that could destroy Devereaux's empire.

Mason felt a thrill as the final pieces fell into place. The smoking gun was near.

They were racing toward the truth, and for the first time, there was light at the end of the track.

# CHAPTER EIGHT

Jack approached Mason with some information. He had heard about a mysterious figure known as the Ghost Driver. Rumours suggested this driver was involved in criminal dealings. The whispers hinted that he held secret meetings at an old warehouse on the outskirts of town.

Jack thought there could be evidence there. "We have to investigate this warehouse," Mason said. Jack gave him the address: the corner of Seventh and Maple. He asked if Mason wanted him to tag along.

"It's safer if Eva and I go, in an official FBI capacity," Mason replied.

They parked across the street from the warehouse in a small alley. "Let's do a walk round," whispered Eva. "We don't want any surprises again."

They circled the warehouse twice, searching for signs of activity or security systems. Mason couldn't contain his impatience to enter, but Eva held him back.

They found a door on the side of the building, away from the prying eyes on the road. Mason put his shoulder against it and shoved. The door creaked open, groaning on its rusty hinges. As they entered, they moved like shadows, every footstep measured. Silence pressed in, thick and heavy.

Shards of light cut through the windows, allowing just enough visibility without using torches. One step at a time, they ventured further into the warehouse.

They saw a door on the right leading off the main area of the warehouse. It was unlocked and opened into a room filled with Formula One memorabilia.

"Do you see this?" Mason exclaimed. The shelves were filled with dusty trophies and photographs. "Racing was pure once," he murmured, tracing a finger along a faded photograph. "Before greed corrupted it all."

Eva nodded, scanning the shelves. "We need to expose them. Every single one."

They searched the room. A table piled with files and boxes caught their attention.

Mason reached out, picked up a framed photograph, and traced his fingers over the faded image. "This world is gone," he whispered.

They began to read some letters found in an old wooden box.

Eva held a handful of papers. "Mason, look at this. There are references to previous accidents at each track. They were involved in some scheme to rig races, to win big money betting on them."

As she read on, the full extent of the situation sank in. "They're not just sabotaging teams, they're controlling the whole sport."

Mason nodded. "Whoever this Ghost Driver and the head honchos are, they're planning something far beyond what we imagined. They want power, and they'll stop at nothing to get it."

The room felt smaller, the stakes larger. They were up against a web of corruption that reached higher than they feared.

The duo returned to the mountain of files, trying to uncover more pieces of the puzzle. With each message deciphered, they glimpsed the twisted mentality of the Ghost Driver.

"We're getting closer to unravelling this mystery," Eva said. New connections formed in Mason's mind. The evidence painted a sprawling network of power, and they had barely scratched the surface.

"I think we have something big here," Mason said.

Eva nodded. "These clues mean we are heading in the right direction."

Both fell silent as the realisation hit. "We have to bring them down," Mason said. "We can't watch them manipulate Formula One any longer."

"Exactly. Gather enough evidence, and we end this empire of corruption," Eva added. "By tracing money trails, identifying accounts, and connecting the dots, we have a watertight case."

Just then, Eva heard a noise outside. "Mason, there's someone out there!" They quickly collected as much information as possible.

Shadows moved, footsteps grew louder. Eva whispered, "They're inside, Mason. How did they know we were onto them?"

He clutched the files closer. "Keep working," he murmured. "We must take as much evidence as possible."

They resumed gathering files at a faster pace, careful in the shadows as footsteps echoed outside.

Mason whispered urgently, "We need to move. Now." Eva nodded.

They searched for an escape route, moving past columns of used tyres and scrambling over engine parts strewn across the floor. Adrenaline surged through their veins.

As they reached the door, flashlight beams cut through the darkness. Mason and Eva froze, locking eyes for a split second before springing into action.

"Go!" Mason yelled, yanking the back door open into the alley. Eva sprinted forward, graceful and fast. Mason followed, struggling to match her pace.

Shouts echoed in the narrow alleyways as pursuers closed in.

"We can't let them catch us," Eva said, vaulting a fallen crate.

"We won't!" Mason's legs burned, driven by sheer determination.

They ran until reaching the car, adrenaline surging. Jumping in, they slammed the doors shut and sped away.

In the rear-view mirror, shadowy figures lingered before melting into the darkness.

"Whoever they are," Mason said, "they won't stop us from uncovering the truth."

They drove for miles, employing anti-surveillance tactics: stopping at odd times, doubling back, and memorising registration plates.

Arriving at headquarters, they laid out the seized files on the table.

Mason received threatening texts from a new number. "They must know we're close to blowing this wide open," he said.

Eva's face was set firmly. "We won't back down."

Mason admired her resolve. She was his rock, pushing him forward.

Every second counted. Armed with evidence, Mason knew they could topple those responsible.

"We have everything we need," Mason said quietly, cramming files into a duffle bag. "It's time to blow the whistle."

Eva nodded solemnly. "The world must know what's been happening. We owe it to everyone affected."

They silently acknowledged the step ahead. They left their base, ready for whatever lay in wait.

Justice was within reach, and the shadow over racing might finally lift.

# CHAPTER NINE

Mason Trevallion stared at the brown paper package in his hands. Sent without a return address, it filled his gut with a cold, tightening knot. The edges were frayed, evidence of a long, rough journey. He carefully opened the package, revealing what lay inside.

Eva moved closer. "What do you think it might be?"

"I really don't know." His fingers trembled slightly as he reached into it.

He brought out a bundle of faded letters and sepia-toned photos.

Mason squinted and scratched his head. He picked up a photograph, turned it over, and held it to the light.

Fragments of memory uncoiled inside him, faces and places flooding back in uneven waves. A cold unease crept through him.

One photo caught his eye: himself as a boy standing next to a sleek racing car. That image, innocence beside speed and danger, had shaped more of him than he'd ever admitted.

Eva laid her hand on Mason's shoulder. "Do you think this is somehow linked to the sabotage?" she asked softly.

Mason's eyes hardened as he nodded slowly. "There has to be some kind of connection," he replied. "Whoever sent this package wants me to understand what happened back then.

We need to go back to my old stomping ground," he said quietly.

"Are you sure?" Eva asked.

"Yeah, learning about my past might shed some light on what we're dealing with now."

Determined, Mason convinced Eva that returning home was their only way forward. They mapped the journey, a quiet urgency lingering between them.

As they pulled into town, Mason began to feel an old anxiety tightening beneath his skin. Nostalgia was a strong emotion, and he swore he could smell freshly cut grass even before he stepped out of the car. Memories came back as they walked along the streets, and Eva could sense his apprehension.

Passing half-forgotten landmarks triggered fragments of long-lost moments: the playground echoing with laughter, the schoolyard where he'd raced his friends. The playground where he'd spent hours with friends echoes of his younger self laughing.

They stopped at the park. Mason stood staring at the broken-down racetrack.

"Are you all right?" Eva asked. "You seem far away."

"Yeah, this place has so many memories," Mason answered. "I didn't think it would be so emotional coming back here. I've forgotten much of my childhood, maybe even blocked it out."

Eva nodded. "Sometimes when we revisit history, it brings us to places we thought we'd moved on from," she said quietly.

Their path took them along a street of small shops: a bakery, a sweet shop, a butcher's and a barber's. Then, they turned left and walked down a leafy avenue.

Mason suddenly stopped.

Wedged between two giant oak trees was an old, dilapidated garage. Harper's Auto Repairs, according to the sign hanging above the door.

Mason hesitated before pushing the door open and stepping inside. He found himself in a shrine to the past: dusty trophies, faded photographs, and oil-stained rags scattered among relics of bygone engines.

An old man, grizzled from years of hard work, stepped from behind a stack of tyres. He squinted at Mason and Eva. "Can I help you? I'm the owner, Jim Harper," he said with a gravelled voice.

Mason stepped forward, his voice steady despite the tremor. "I hope so," he replied. "I stayed in this town many years ago. I'm looking for answers about my past. My brother and father were heavily involved in racing back then."

Jim let his gaze sweep over the young man before a flicker of recognition crossed his face. "You're a Trevallion," he stated, then softly, "You look just like your mother."

Mason nodded gravely. "That's correct," he replied. "Someone sent me letters and photos from my childhood. I've returned to figure out what it all means."

Jim sighed deeply, motioning them towards a cramped office lined with racing posters faded and curling at the edges.

Mason felt queasy. Every nerve hummed with dread. Whatever truths were coming his way could change everything he knew about his past.

"So, then," Jim began, his voice heavy with remorse, "you'll want to hear about the accident. That's what set you off, going all wacky and leaving town. Your parents just said you were staying with relatives."

Mason's heart pounded. "Yes," he whispered.

Jim hesitated, weighing how much truth the young man could bear. Mason's gaze didn't waver.

"Your dad and brother were involved in our local racing scene for years. They were doing quite well and making a name for themselves."

Mason listened intently. The words were hazy, echoing through the fog of half-buried memories. He needed the gaps filled in, no matter how painful.

"There was an open race that your brother had entered," Jim continued. "It was an event that was attracting some major sponsors, so your brother looked at it as an opportunity to showcase his skills. Your dad had put his heart and soul into making sure the car was pieced together exactly right. It was a beautiful machine and lightning fast."

As the mechanic spoke, Mason's mind replayed flickering images: heat shimmering off the tarmac, engines roaring, his father's grease-streaked grin.

"It all went to hell," Jim murmured. "He started to lose control around one of the corners, picked up speed and flipped over onto his side. He collided with another car. The impact was brutal."

Suddenly, an image came to Mason. His mother's hand gripped his wrist, dragging him through the chaos. Smoke. Screams. The metallic tang of burning fuel.

He'd cried out, not from pain, but from confusion, as the world dissolved into noise and flame.

"The crash was so severe that the other car smashed into the safety barrier. Your brother's car overturned and went up in flames," Jim explained. "By the time anybody reached your brother, nothing could be done. There was no chance."

Tears welled up in Mason's eyes until his vision blurred with grief. He remembered being at a funeral, but as a child, he hadn't understood what was going on.

That day had splintered his family beyond repair, a wound that had never scabbed over.

No one had ever spoken of it again. His mother's silence became accusation, his father's workaholic obsession, penance.

# CHAPTER TEN

"There's more," Jim continued. "Other people were involved: a local cattle rancher, his wife and daughter, powerful figures who held sway over the local racing circuit. When the report by the crash investigators was released to the public, it was deemed just an unfortunate accident. However, there remained one strong rumour: the rancher had allegedly bribed the investigator, suggesting that what happened might not have been a simple accident."

Mason stared at Jim, his throat tightening, disbelief flaring behind his eyes. This was the first he had heard of it. "Why?" The question burst from him, raw anger.

Jim shook his head slowly. "I don't know all the details," he admitted. "Rumours were swirling around like sagebrush caught in a tornado. Someone said your dad had crossed paths with the Devereaux family when he was setting up his garage for your brother's racing car. Another rumour claimed your brother was on the verge of securing a major sponsorship that could have launched him into the big leagues."

Mason cut him off, "Devereaux?" He flinched at the mention of that name. Could Lucas Devereaux's family be tied to his brother's death?

Anger ignited in Mason's chest, burning away the shock. The people behind the sabotage had got away with murder, his brother's murder.

Eva reached out and clasped his trembling hand, offering the quiet steadiness he couldn't summon alone.

"We won't let this go," Mason said, voice low but firm. "We need to find proof of a connection between my brother's death and the recent accidents."

They sat in silence.

"I need to know more," Mason said. "Who is this big fish? What is his connection to our sabotage cases?"

Jim winced slightly, his eyes darting between Mason and Eva. He hesitated, fear flickering in his eyes, a fear that speaking out might be digging his own grave.

Jim admitted in a low tone, "The Devereaux family is still the big shot around town, and I don't have all the answers. However, I do know there's a lot of history with them in racing, along with plenty of rumours about shady dealings."

Mason tried to make sense of things, and Eva could see his brow furrowing. "So, they used their power and money to manipulate the races and win?" he asked.

"Yes, but it went further than that," Jim said gravely. "They had a bigger agenda, a desire for control and dominance over everyone. Those recent acts of sabotage you told me about sound very similar to what happened all those years ago. Your brother wasn't the only one who suffered a suspicious accident."

Eva leaned forward. "And what about the Ghost Driver? What role does he play in all of this?"

Jim sighed and looked down at the floor. "I really can't say," he replied. "This Ghost Driver scares the daylights out of me. He's ruthless and relentless."

"We need to know who he is," Mason said. "If we expose him, it might be the key to bringing the whole conspiracy down."

Eva pressed, "Who is he?" Her voice rose with expectation.

Jim cast a glance around the room as though he expected someone to be listening, then drew closer. "There used to be a driver named Roberto Silva. He was supposed to be one of the greatest out there before an accident brought an early end to his career."

As soon as he mentioned Silva, Mason's ears pricked up. "What happened?" he asked, his tone sharpening.

That made Jim shift uncomfortably in his chair. "Well, Silva had races where things kept breaking down; he couldn't explain what had happened. Then he had a terrible accident. He walked away with his life but suffered severe injuries that hospitalised him for months. When he was released, he couldn't face racing again. Some say he lost his nerve and was never the same. Things like that tend to stay with you."

What Jim had just described was chillingly familiar. An echo of the same sabotage Mason had faced.

Mason shared a look with Eva. "Sounds familiar, doesn't it, Eva?"

"Where can we find Silva?" Eva asked.

Jim hesitated for a moment but relented with a resigned sigh. "The last thing I heard, Silva was off the grid," he finally gave in. "People say that he might be hiding out near the abandoned racetrack on the edge of town."

"We'll find him, no matter where he is," said Mason, his tone hardening, eyes set on the horizon. "We'll uncover the truth for everyone affected by this sabotage."

As they left Jim's garage, Mason felt something fierce and determined ignite inside him. Eva noticed this but knew the road ahead would be filled with danger. Finding Silva could be the key, but it might also unlock something darker.

The desert wind howled across the empty lot where the makeshift racetrack stood, the cracked road surface baking under the Nevada sun. Six-year-old Mason Trevallion crouched behind a stack of tyres, his fingers tracing the grooves in the rubber as he watched his older brother, Daniel, tinker with the engine of their father's old stock car.

"C'mon, Danny, let me help!" Mason begged, rocking on his heels, impatient.

Daniel grinned, wiping grease from his hands onto jeans already heavy with stains. "You'll get your turn, squirt. But today's my race. Big sponsors are watching."

Mason's chest swelled with pride. Daniel was already a local legend, the kid who outdrove men twice his age in back-alley dirt races. Their dad, a former mechanic, poured every dime into Daniel's career, betting everything on his success.

"You're gonna win," Mason declared.

Daniel ruffled his hair. "Damn right. And when I'm in Formula One, you'll be my pit crew."

The track was packed with people, rare for amateur night. Men in suits lingered near the pit wall, their eyes sharp.

The lights blinked on one by one. Then darkness. The race began.

Daniel's car launched like a bullet, the roar of its V8 drowning the crowd. The pack funnelled into Turn one, a snarling beast of smoking tyres and side-by-side chaos. Daniel rode the high line, tyres kissing the wall as he sliced past two cars before the back straight.

Mason pressed his face to the chain-link fence, his heart pounding in time with every rev.

Lap eight. Daniel was pulling away, his car a black streak under the floodlights.

Then ... a metallic SNAP on turn nine.

A sharp left, banked at 22 degrees. Daniel took it flat-out, no lift, just like always. But this time, something went wrong.

The rear suspension buckled. The car snapped sideways, tyres screeching in agony. For one horrifying second, it balanced on two wheels, then pirouetted into a roll, and flipped.

Daniel's car slammed roof-first into another, throwing it into the barrier. A fireball erupted, and Daniel's car burst into flames.

Mason's world went silent.

The hospital smelled of antiseptic and grief. Mason pressed his face against the intensive care unit window, watching his father sob into his hands. His mother hadn't spoken for hours.

"Mechanical failure," the officials said. "Freak accident."

That night, he crept into the garage, where the wreck sat like a corpse. His father held a piece of suspension. "A clean cut, not a break. It was sabotage," his father whispered. Then he shook his head. "Ain't nothing we can do."

Mason didn't understand.

The next morning, the car was gone. Sold for scrap.

Danny had the gift. Everyone said it. His reflexes, his calm, the way he coaxed speed out of a machine like he whispered to it. Mason was just the little brother, lemonade in hand, wide-eyed at the pit wall.

Until the accident.

No one spoke about it, or Danny.

At the funeral, Mason stared at Danny's helmet, scuffed and battle-worn, resting on the casket. When the dirt hit the wood, Mason asked his mother if Danny was in heaven. She burst into tears and crushed him against her chest.

Mason's family was shattered. His mother sent him to live with an uncle. His father eventually drank himself into oblivion.

Mason's life was reduced to drudgery on his uncle's farm.

Until the county fair. His twelfth birthday.

A makeshift go-kart track caught his eye, just tyres and plywood. Mason begged five bucks off his uncle for a turn.

The kart was nothing but a lawnmower engine bolted to a steel frame. But when Mason stomped the throttle and the machine lurched forward, something lit inside him. It wasn't just speed, it was clarity. The noise, the vibration, the weightlessness in corners. It clicked.

He didn't just drive; he attacked. Other kids bumbled, laughing, bumping tyres. Mason cut lines, leaned into apexes, feathered the brake like he was born doing it. When the chequered flag fell, he wasn't just first, he was half a lap ahead.

The track owner noticed. He let Mason hang around, sweeping floors and wiping helmets in exchange for extra laps. Mason studied every angle, every throttle input. He memorised the sound of grip, knowing when it was understeer and when it was oversteer. By fourteen, he ran laps men couldn't touch.

Racing costs money. Money his relatives didn't have. So Mason learned to wrench.

He scavenged parts, traded labour for scrap tyres and begged old racers for advice. Every bolt he turned was armour against the helplessness of Danny's death.

By sixteen, the kart track felt too small. Too tame. And then he found the streets.

The night was another beast entirely. Out by the old airstrip, the desert air tasted like gasoline and danger. Cars lined up like soldiers, imports, domestics, gutted shells, tuned monsters. The air buzzed with money, testosterone, and nitrous hiss.

That's where Mason saw his first Camaro. A beat-up '69 shell with primer paint, no chrome, just menace. He knew he had to have it.

He hustled a summer at the junkyard, cutting deals, stacking parts. By fall, the Camaro was his. And he turned it into a weapon. Out went the tired V8; in went a Corvette LS7 pulled from a wreck. He dropped the chassis low, stiffened suspension, bolted slicks on the back that clung to pavement like claws.

When he fired it up, the camshaft's throb rattled his bones. He hadn't just built a car; he'd built a machine to carry him where Danny never went.

Mason's first street race was chaos. Only headlights marked the line, flickering against the cracked runway. The smell of burnt rubber hung heavy. Cash swapped hands like poker chips.

Mason lined up against a Mustang, its blown V8 whining like a banshee. The starter dropped his arms.

Mason's Camaro clawed at the ground, rear end twitching. His heart pounded like a jackhammer. The Mustang jumped ahead, tyres screaming. Mason slammed into second, the LS7 roared, and suddenly the world narrowed to a tunnel of speed. Third gear. The Camaro surged forward. The Mustang blurred in the rearview.

The crowd roared, but Mason didn't hear. Only Danny's laugh carried in the wind, urging him on.

When he crossed the line, money flew, fists pumped, and Mason just sat there, breathing hard, hands trembling on the wheel.

The boy was gone; in his place sat a racer reborn in fire and speed.

# CHAPTER ELEVEN

Word spread. The kid in the Camaro was fast. Too fast.

He ran every weekend against Supras, RX-7s, and tuned-up Civics with turbos that screamed like jet engines.

He learned to read opponents: who had traction, who had lag, who cracked under pressure. He gambled small at first, then larger.

And he won.

But speed had a price. Cops raided the meets. Friends crashed. One night a Mitsubishi Evo flipped end-over-end, the driver crawling out bloodied, screaming as the car burned.

Mason helped drag him clear, the heat blistering his skin. He didn't sleep for two nights. Nightmares of Danny's crash came back in vivid flashes.

Still, he returned. Each race pulled him back because every time he raced, he felt closer to Danny.

At the old airstrip, the Camaro sat low, exhaust snarling, headlights dark. Across from him, a Nissan GT-R gleamed silver, twin-turbo, titanium everything.

The driver leaned out, smirking. "You're just a kid."

Mason grinned, foot hovering over the clutch. "And you're about to choke on my exhaust fumes."

The flag dropped.

The Camaro launched, tyres spitting sparks, torque slamming Mason into the seat. The GT-R hesitated, with turbo lag, giving Mason a head start.

That night wasn't just a win. It was a declaration.

Among the crowd was Alvarez. Retired racer. Scarred hands, sharp eyes. He saw something in Mason. Not just recklessness, but talent.

"You ever think about going legit?" Alvarez asked, flipping Mason a business card.

Mason laughed. "Can't afford it."

"Maybe you can't afford not to."

That conversation changed everything.

Alvarez got Mason a test day at a local circuit with real race cars. Mason slid into the seat and drove like his life depended on it. His lines were raw, aggressive, but blisteringly quick.

Team owners noticed. Doors began to open.

Alvarez shoved him into junior leagues, hustling sponsors, calling in favours. Mason scraped by on borrowed engines, second-hand tyres, sleeping in vans between races. But he kept winning.

From junior leagues, he moved to Formula Ford. Then Formula 3. Each step harder, faster, more brutal. Racing in Europe was a battlefield, but Mason thrived. His Camaro nights forged him in fire, late braking, wheel-to-wheel combat, split-second guts.

*Monza. Silverstone. Spa.* Circuits that chewed up rookies and spat them out. Mason bled for every tenth of a second. He spun out in the rain but always clawed forward.

He earned a reputation: fearless, sometimes reckless, but with a killer instinct. Rivals hated going wheel-to-wheel with him. He'd dive into impossible gaps, daring others to blink first. Most did.

By 2009, Mason was in Formula 2, the final proving ground. He knew he was the fastest driver on the grid, just cursed with bad luck. He won when he finished. When he didn't finish, he'd crash spectacularly.

Still too aggressive, still raw, but undeniably fast. He sat 4th in the championship mid-season.

That's when he got the call. Against the odds, he was offered a seat for the 2010 Formula One season.

Australia, 2010. The grid buzzed with tension. Mason sat in the cockpit, heart hammering, hands clamped on the wheel. The lights above blinked red. Engines screamed around him, Ferraris, McLarens, Mercedes, Renault, and Williams Cosworth, monsters worth millions.

The lights went out.

Mason launched, instincts taking over. He dived into Turn One, three-wide, brakes smoking, tyres clawing asphalt. Carbon fibre splintered. Mason threaded the chaos, adrenaline flooding him.

Lap after lap, he wrestled the car, every corner a knife's edge. He wasn't just driving, he was surviving.

By the chequered flag, he wasn't on the podium. But he finished. And that mattered.

Because Mason wasn't there just for points. He was there for the ghost of his brother.

Every lap, he felt Danny. Watching. Smiling. Riding shotgun in the roar of the engine.

And Mason knew one thing: he'd never stop chasing.

His first season in Formula One was everything he'd dreamed and more. Adrenaline. Glamour. Money, more money than he'd ever imagined. Private jets to Monaco, handshakes with royalty and celebrities.

The fans were intoxicating. Crowds screamed his name. Girls crowded for a glimpse, an autograph, a chance to slip him a number. Cameras flashed everywhere. Interviewers lined up to hear about the street kid who clawed his way into Formula One. Mason wasn't just a driver now; he was a myth.

And Mason believed it.

At first, it was harmless. A night out in Monte Carlo, clubs so exclusive you needed a six-figure watch just to enter. Dom Pérignon lined tables. Women with diamond eyes and designer gowns leaned close, laughing at every word Mason said. He was twenty-five, fast, rich, untouchable.

But the lines soon blurred. Nights out bled into mornings. Hangovers stretched into afternoons. And the casinos, God, the casinos.

Monaco was the worst. The place glittered like a mirage, and Mason fell hard. The roulette wheel spun, and with it, his balance. At first, he won enough to stay hooked. Twenty grand in a night, easy money, he thought. But then the house collected. Thirty, fifty, seventy thousand gone in a night, and Mason barely blinked. He'd win it back on Sunday, he told himself. He always did.

But this time, he didn't.

The losses piled. The debts whispered through the paddock. Sponsors noticed. His team noticed. Mason shrugged it off with a grin and another drink in hand.

The women blurred into one another. He paraded models like trophies, swapping them as easily as tyres. Gossip magazines ate it up. Mason Trevallion, Formula One's bad boy.

On track, cracks showed. Late to practice sessions. Hungover in the simulator. Reflexes dulled; braking a fraction late, missing apexes he once carved like a surgeon. His temper flared, shouting at engineers, blaming everyone but himself.

Carlos Morales, his race engineer, saw it unravel in real time. After debriefs, he'd pull Mason aside, voice low, steady, the way you talk to someone teetering on a cliff.

"You're burning the candle at both ends, Mason. Keep this up and you'll crash, on or off the track."

Mason would laugh, clap him on the shoulder. "Relax, Carlos. I've got it under control. I always do."

But Carlos wasn't laughing. He'd seen drivers self-destruct before. He knew the signs. Recklessness. Bravado. Hollow eyes behind the charm. Mason was a firework, bright, fast, doomed to explode.

Then came Montreal.

A Friday night bender bled straight into Saturday practice. Mason climbed into the cockpit still reeking of whiskey, eyes bloodshot, hands shaking on the wheel. He clipped the barrier on his out-lap, wrecking the car before he'd even set a time. The team boss was livid. Sponsors threatened to pull out. Carlos found him later, slumped in the team motorhome, half-asleep with a glass in his hand.

"This isn't you," Carlos said, voice breaking. "This is the booze talking. Mason, you're throwing it all away."

Mason barely looked up. "I'm fine. Just a bad day."

But it wasn't just a day. It was a pattern.

The final straw came at Monza. Mason had been warned. Curfews were strict, regulations ironclad. But he blew it off, sneaking out to Milan, poker games, vodka shots until sunrise. He rolled into the paddock late, still drunk, cameras capturing him stumbling. The footage went viral within hours.

The FIA stepped in. His team had no choice. Mid-season, the announcement dropped: Mason Trevallion's contract terminated. The rookie sensation was finished.

The press tore him apart. "Wasted Talent." "Playboy Implodes." "From Street Racer to Street Trash." Headlines cut sharper than any crash. The fans who once screamed his name now jeered.

And Mason? He went silent. For the first time in his life, he had no grin, no bravado. Just an empty hotel room, a bottle of whiskey, and the crushing realisation he'd thrown it all away.

He might not have survived, had it not been for Carlos.

Carlos didn't give up. He showed up at Mason's door, dragged him out of bed, and forced him to face himself. No excuses. No running.

He sat Mason down and laid it out clearly: "You can drink yourself into oblivion, gamble until you're broke, sleep your way across Europe until no one remembers your name, or you can fight. You can turn it around. But you've got to decide now. Right now."

It wasn't easy. Rehab. Counselling. Months in the shadows, rebuilding not just his body but his mind. Mason fought cravings, demons, and the urge to drown in loss. Carlos stayed, the steady hand, the anchor that kept him from drifting into nothing.

Slowly, Mason clawed back.

Not to Formula One. That door was shut.

But to life. To purpose.

Carlos pushed him toward discipline, structure, something beyond the track. He called in favours, pulling strings that landed Mason a place at Quantico as an FBI candidate. The chance came like a lifeline. The speed, the danger, the adrenaline, still there, but now with a cause worth fighting for.

Mason took it, burning with the need to prove he wasn't just another fallen star.

He owed Carlos everything. Without him, Mason knew he'd be another obituary of wasted talent. Instead, he had a second chance.

And Mason didn't intend to waste it.

# CHAPTER TWELVE

Mason pulled a photo from his wallet. His brother stared back at him from the photo he'd carried for twenty years. The cycle of sabotage and corruption was repeating itself.

They sat in silence for a while before Mason spoke, voice low and uneven. "I haven't talked about my brother with anyone in years, ever since I was a kid. My parents kept everything from me and never really told me what happened," he said. "That's why they were so against me starting to race. There was always a bad feeling in our family. They suggested I leave and go live with my aunt and uncle." He continued, "Mum and Dad never came to see me when I started racing. That hurt more than any crash I've been in."

The memories rose unbidden, sharp and piercing. "I was always a bit headstrong back then and made some impulsive decisions. What I need now, though, is to know the truth. I need justice for everything that has happened to my family. They both died without me knowing the full story; otherwise, I could have put things right between us."

Very rarely had Mason shown this level of emotion. His voice cracked, the old restraint giving way to raw regret. She reached out and hugged him tightly. When he finally pulled back, his eyes were rimmed red but resolute.

"Thanks for your support," he sighed. "But, we need to find Silva, that's our top priority."

Eva started the car and sped out of the parking lot, determined to find the elusive driver, Roberto Silva.

They took a left turn and then another, driving down an old, deserted dirt road. As they rounded a bend, the abandoned racetrack came into view. It loomed like a ghost from his past, offering both answers and danger.

They parked the car at a padlocked gate. A sign read *'Private Property - No Unauthorised Access'.*

Sitting in the car, they stared at the track. "It kind of gives me the creeps," Eva whispered, low enough not to shatter the silence surrounding them.

Mason nodded, his eyes scanning, searching for any sign of life. "It's like time has just stopped," he commented. Suddenly, he slapped his palms on the dashboard. "Let's do this; let's go find Silva," he declared.

The old padlock didn't take much persuasion before it snapped open. They walked through the racetrack entrance, boots crunching over gravel and broken glass. Every step echoed their shared hope and the danger lurking in the silence.

They stepped onto the crumbling asphalt, dust curling around their ankles like pale smoke, footsteps echoing off hollow stands.

Mason peered into the darkness, looking for Silva. "I hope Silva can answer some of my questions."

Eva nodded, her hand resting lightly on the gun in her holster. "Keep your senses keen," she warned. "You never know what's hiding out there in the darkness."

They continued down the track. An engine roared to life, sudden and sharp, splitting the quiet. They turned toward the sound and saw a figure emerging from one of the garages. He strode towards them with a shotgun in his hand.

The figure stopped a few feet from them and looked intently at them. "What do you want here?" he growled, the shotgun pointing menacingly at them.

Mason stepped forward, "My name is Mason Trevallion," and extended his hand in a friendly gesture. "This is my partner Eva. We're looking for Roberto Silva."

Silva considered Mason's words, assessing his intentions. "Are you two cops?" he asked. "Hang on, Trevallion, that name sounds familiar," he said.

"My family used to live in town several years ago, and I had a season racing in Formula One," Mason explained. "Maybe that's where you've heard of me? Maybe you could lower the shotgun so we can talk? We're looking for information on a guy known as the Ghost Driver."

"You're better off steering clear of him," replied Silva. "He's bad news, but I'll help you in any way I can." Silva lowered the shotgun. "Follow me; we can talk in the office. Oh, and sorry about the hardware. I don't get many visitors here, and you can't be too careful these days."

Inside the office, walls plastered with yellowed photographs and oil-stained newspaper clippings told their own history, Silva's glory days and the fall that followed.

"We're here to get answers," Mason responded firmly. "What do you know about the Ghost Driver?"

Silva looked down, the shadows in the room deepening around him. "He's a legend in the worst way," he said slowly. "People say he's not even human anymore, that the crash twisted him inside out, body and mind. The Ghost Driver is what's left when you strip away a man's soul."

"You're saying he's... supernatural?" Eva asked sceptically.

Silva shook his head. "No. He's flesh and blood. But he's driven by some unholy revenge. After my accident, I started hearing whispers about a driver who'd returned from the brink. He wore a black helmet, never spoke, and raced only at night. They said he was unbeatable."

Mason spoke quietly, disbelief edged with fascination. "And you think this driver is behind the sabotage?"

"I don't think," Silva said grimly. "I know. I saw him once. At a rally years after my crash, he showed up unannounced and took to the track. He destroyed every car that tried to pass him. When the race was over, he disappeared, vanished into the smoke."

Eva's brow furrowed. "That's impossible."

Silva looked up sharply. "You think I imagined it? You think I'd mistake a ghost for a man?" He leaned across the desk. "That night, when the smoke cleared, I found something in the dirt: a piece of metal from his car, engraved with the Devereaux family logo."

Mason's stomach dropped. "Devereaux again."

# CHAPTER THIRTEEN

"We all knew the Ghost Driver rigged his races to guarantee victory. He was investigated many times, but his influential friends buried any scandal that threatened his name. Secret alliances, betrayals, and power struggles fuelled his rise and cemented his dominance."

"Why?" Mason asked, "What do they hope to gain from all this?" Silva stared past him for a moment, weighing the question. "Well, it's all about control," he replied solemnly. "If he can create enough chaos in the sport, no one will challenge his dominance."

"We cannot allow this," Eva stated. "We need to expose the Ghost Driver and bring down this reign of terror."

Silva nodded grimly. "It's not going to be an easy task. He won't give up without a fight."

"We're ready," Mason said firmly. "Between the evidence we've gathered and what you've told us, it's enough to take down the Ghost Driver and his entire network."

The revelation strengthened Mason's belief that they were closer than ever to bringing everyone to justice.

As they walked away from the deserted track, Mason felt a rare surge of triumph. With Silva as another formidable ally, they were ready to confront the Ghost Driver.

The following day, Roberto Silva was waiting for Mason and Eva outside their office. "What's the plan today, boss?" he asked.

"Let's get into the office first," Eva replied with a faint grin.

Just as they reached the door, Mason received another anonymous tip: the Ghost Driver would be meeting with one of his mysterious benefactors.

"What is it this time?" Eva asked. "Another tip-off?"

"The Ghost Driver is meeting one of his rich and powerful cronies," Mason replied.

"Who's tipping you off?" Silva inquired.

Eva cut in, "We have an insider, they have their finger on the pulse and have been feeding us information now and again to keep us on the right track."

"OK, let's get organised and crash this meeting," said Silva.

They arrived early, scouting the building's entrances and exits; there was only one. They now sat in a café overlooking the building entrance.

Eva murmured, "That guy in the dark jacket and baseball cap has passed the entrance three times now."

"I've been watching and haven't seen him before," Silva said, narrowing his eyes.

"Different hat, different jacket... check out the sneakers. Very distinctive, aren't they? I have an eye for detail!" she replied. Sure enough, when the stranger reached the entrance, he slipped inside.

They left the café and slipped into the building unnoticed, gathering in the sparsely lit reception area. The sound of dripping water echoed through the corridor ahead. They opened the door and entered a large conference room.

Mason felt his pulse quicken. This was their only chance to take down the Ghost Driver and one of his masters.

"Stay close," Eva whispered. "We don't know what jiggery-pokery these mobsters have up their sleeves."

They inched further into the room. Whispers echoed ahead, growing louder with every cautious step. Suddenly, a door opened and out walked the man in sneakers.

This had to be the Ghost Driver.

Mason knew he'd seen him before, and recognition flared in the stranger's eyes too.

"This is where the game ends," Mason declared. "You have caused enough chaos and havoc."

The Ghost Driver chuckled darkly. "Do you think you can stop me?" he taunted. "You tried before and failed. I am like a phantom."

Eva stepped forward. "We know what you're up to," she said firmly. "Your need for control and dominance will bring you down."

Silva interjected, "We'll stop you here. The only thing left for you is to tell us who your partners are. Your days of destroying lives are over."

The Ghost Driver let out a laugh. "You couldn't stop me before, Silva, and you won't stop me now. I am an unstoppable force."

In a blur, the Ghost Driver lunged forward, lightning fast, his movements sharp and deadly.

Silva stepped forward. "I've got this. He's mine, Mason. There's a debt to settle here," he said, and hurled himself at his old enemy.

The fight erupted. Punches flew, fists cracking against bones. Kicks landed hard, each man trading brutal strikes.

Mason knew this was the same man he'd fought in the secret room; he tensed, ready to intervene if Silva faltered.

Silva and the Ghost Driver circled each other like predators, locked in a deadly rhythm. Silva drew on his street-fighting, anticipating and countering each move with ruthless precision.

The Ghost Driver's confidence wavered as he realised that Silva was outmatching him. The more punches and kicks he threw at Silva, the more he got back.

Silva knew he had him reeling. With a spinning leg sweep, he sent the Ghost Driver crashing to the floor and moved in for the finishing blow. He raised his arm for a throat strike, a lethal move that would end it.

"No, Silva, don't. We want him alive; he needs to pay for his crimes," shouted Mason.

The Ghost Driver's shoulders drooped, and Silva pulled him up into a sitting position for questioning. He revealed how the sabotages were carried out.

He said he'd been given electronic devices and told where to plant them in the cars. He had been equipped with a small remote control to trigger them.

He just had to wait for the right time, and BOOM, the car would either blow up or the driver would lose control.

He told them the devices were advanced pieces of technology that could manipulate multiple performance systems in the race cars. He didn't know who made them, only that Lucas Devereaux had given them to him.

When Mason and Silva loosened their grip and their questioning, he realised it was his chance to bolt.

He made his break, but Eva spotted him. She charged and tackled him to the ground, pinning him with a thud till Mason and Silva rushed to assist.

Mason narrowed his eyes. "Is that everything? Don't leave anything out."

The Ghost Driver hesitated, eyes darting wildly. Finally, he relented. "OK, I'll give you names," he said. "In return for some sort of plea bargain."

He paused, then continued, "But you'll never bring down the whole organisation. This goes deeper than you can comprehend."

The Ghost Driver named everyone involved in the sabotage and those entangled in the corruption and deceit.

"We will do what we can. Regardless of the size or strength of the organisation, we will fight them until justice is served," Mason said quietly.

"We have sufficient proof to act now," Eva said. "It's time to dismantle the empire and arrest the remaining conspirators."

They walked away from the building, knowing that the Ghost Driver's reign of terror had ended.

"I'll drive; you can sit in the back with him," Eva said, nodding towards the Ghost Driver. Silva took his place in the front seat next to Eva. They would drop the Ghost Driver off at the nearest FBI office for further questioning.

They would now take down all those who had poisoned the industry with deceit and corruption.

# CHAPTER FOURTEEN

Lucas Devereaux held a meeting for the press and public at the racetrack. He stood before the gathered crowd, confidence radiating as he aimed to prove that Racing Shadows was unshaken.

Mason and Eva arrived, weaving through the press of bodies. As they neared him, the crowd thickened, forming a restless sea of onlookers straining to catch a glimpse of Devereaux.

As they closed in, Mason's thoughts flashed through the evidence they'd uncovered and the innocent lives Lucas had wrecked. Anger burned inside him, hardening his resolve for justice.

Only feet away, Eva stood, her gaze focussed on Lucas. Her eyes dared him to look away.

Mason took a deep breath and shouted, "Lucas Devereaux, it's time to answer for your crimes." His voice cut through the murmurs.

A murmur swept across the crowd; every eye was now fixed on them.

Mason caught a flash of surprise on Lucas's face before he masked it with a well-rehearsed sneer.

Lucas shrugged with mocking ease. "More investigators trying to dig up secrets that are none of your concern?"

Mason met his glare head-on. "We know everything, Lucas," he said firmly. "Your reign of sabotage is over."

Eva stepped forward, her eyes ablaze. "You honestly thought you could destroy other people's lives and walk away? We're here to drag every one of your schemes into the light."

Lucas's lips curved into a sly smile. "You think you have me cornered," he sneered. "But I've always been a step ahead." He scanned the area, eyes calculating. "Have you got my arrest and trial all planned out? What's next?"

Mason's voice was resolute. He glared directly at Lucas. "We'll make sure everyone knows your crimes, every act of sabotage, every lie, every life you've ruined, exposed for all to see."

"You must have thought you were untouchable," Eva added. "But we're here to make sure you face justice."

Lucas laughed, a cold, sharp sound that sliced through the tension. "Justice? There's no justice. Only power, and those bold enough to seize it."

"Truth's harder to kill than you think," Mason countered, holding his temper. "It always surfaces."

Eva moved closer and whispered to Mason. The crowd leaned in, hungry for the next move.

Lucas grinned. "Truth is simple, but perception is everything. I've spun my web for years. No one can untangle it."

Mason clenched his fists, refusing to back down. "Your web may be intricate, but it's not unbreakable. We've got the proof to shred it."

"This sabotage ends now, Lucas," Eva said. "You're going to pay for every life you've shattered."

The crowd gasped as one. Every eye was fixed on the stand-off.

Lucas's confident expression faltered. His gaze darted between them, the mask slipping to reveal a flicker of fear.

Then a voice cut through the murmurs. Natalie Lindburg forced her way forward. "Lucas Devereaux," she shouted, "today marks the end of your corruption. I have an editorial ready to go live across every major outlet and feed. Your empire will crumble."

Natalie's arrival reminded Mason they weren't alone. They stood as a united front.

As she spoke, the murmurs swelled. Mason felt the tide shift, with the crowd turning against Devereaux.

At last, Lucas's bravado cracked. His shoulders sagged as whispers became chants of outrage.

With a final act of defiance, Lucas spun on his heel and forced his way through the mob. Mason and Eva lunged after him.

Lucas sprinted, shoving past onlookers as the crowd parted, predator and prey in motion.

After a brief chase, Lucas found himself cornered in an office within the Racing Shadows garage. He gasped, unfit for the fight, his panic rising with every breath.

Mason faced him. "It's over, Lucas. Your reign of sabotage ends here."

Lucas's eyes darted. He grabbed a spanner, ready to strike.

Eva swept his legs from under him. He crashed to the floor, the spanner clattering away.

He was beaten. Fury gave way to fear.

At Eva's nod, Mason stepped forward and handcuffed him.

The crowd watched in stunned silence, then erupted in applause. Lucas's eyes darted between Mason, Eva, and the sea of faces, still searching for escape.

Mason shoved him forward. "Time to face the consequences, Lucas."

Eva stood firm. "Every life you've wronged will finally see justice."

Doubt flickered across Lucas's face; his defiance drained away. He scanned the crowd, some shouting for justice, others recording history.

Mason seized the moment. "Your reign of corruption ends now, Devereaux!" Cheers thundered from the crowd.

Police pushed through to take Lucas away. Mason turned to Eva and Natalie. "That went better than expected."

They had torn apart an empire of lies. But their work wasn't done; trust needed rebuilding, and reform demanded action.

Surrounded by a cheering crowd, Mason scanned the hopeful faces, ready to keep fighting for the truth.

Natalie would publish the evidence, exposing every name, forcing Formula One to reform. Chaos would follow.

The revelation of Lucas's treachery rocked the industry. Teams distanced themselves overnight.

No secret could stay buried. Their high-speed pursuit of justice had come full circle.

They had exposed corruption. Devereaux and his conspirators would face trial. The Ghost Driver's reign of fear was over.

Ahead lay rebuilding, trust to mend, and reform to forge.

# EPILOGUE

The courtroom buzzed like a live wire, cameras flashing and microphones capturing every word. Mason sat stiffly in the back row, his hands clenched around the edge of the bench. He could feel the weight of every gaze on him, but he kept his eyes forward, watching the drama unfold.

Lucas Devereaux, once untouchable, now sat in the defendant's dock, his face pale and taut. The judge's gavel cracked through the room like thunder. "Sentences are hereby handed down," the official intoned. The men who had orchestrated chaos in the world of Formula One were led away, their protests drowned by the shuffle of boots on marble floors.

Only the Ghost Driver remained, leaning casually against the defence table, a faint smirk on his lips. Mason caught the subtle exchange of glances between him and the prosecutor. A deal had been struck, and he would walk free, but not unscathed, his cooperation the price for his liberty. Mason felt a cold satisfaction. Justice, messy though it might be, had found its mark.

Outside the courthouse, the press descended like a storm. Reporters shouted questions, cameras clicked, and headlines were written in real time. Mason barely noticed. Alex, emerging from protective custody for the first time in weeks, blinked against the sun, clutching his wife's hand.

"You okay?" Mason asked, matching his pace.

Alex nodded, though his jaw was tight. "I think... I just want to sleep for a week."

"Sleep," Mason repeated quietly, a faint smile tugging at his lips. "Yeah. That sounds perfect."

Across the ocean, the warmth of Barbados wrapped around Carlos and Natalie like a welcome embrace. The sand slipped like silk between their toes, the waves glittering under a blazing sun. They laughed as they exchanged rings, the wind tugging playfully at Natalie's veil.

"I can't believe we're actually doing this," Carlos said, brushing a strand of hair from her face.

"Been waiting long enough," Natalie replied, her eyes alight with mischief and love. "Now, let's make everyone jealous."

Back home, Jack, Jim Harper, and Roberto Silva oversaw a different kind of excitement. Their racing academy thrummed with energy: engines revving, tyres screeching, young hopefuls darting around the track like ants. Mason watched from the sidelines, recognising the spark in each trainee, the same fire that had once driven him and his friends.

"It's not just about speed," Jim said, clapping his hands. "It's about control, focus, and heart. Show me your heart!"

Mason caught Eva's hand briefly, squeezing it. "They'll make it," he murmured.

"They'll make it," she echoed, eyes following a trainee as he hurtled down the straight, determination etched across his face.

Weeks later, the rhythm of work returned. Mason and Eva packed lightly, heading for Mason's hometown. The car wound along familiar roads, the landscape shifting from city sprawl to quiet countryside. He felt a tight knot in his chest, anticipation, fear, longing, everything rolled into one.

At the cemetery, the air was cool and still. Mason knelt before his parents' graves, brushing away fallen leaves and laying fresh flowers. Eva stayed a step behind, her presence steady and unspoken.

"I missed you," Mason whispered, voice breaking just slightly. "I needed to do this ... to say goodbye properly."

Eva rested a hand on his shoulder. "You don't have to speak to them. You're here. That's enough."

For the first time in a long while, Mason felt a fragile peace settle over him, the past loosening its grip just enough to let him breathe. The trial was over, the criminals punished, and life, messy, complicated, and unpredictable, moved forward.

Mason gazed at Eva, then at the horizon, where the sun bled gold across the hills. "We're going to be alright," he said, more to himself than anyone else.

"Yes," Eva replied softly. "We are."

The End

# AUTHOR BIO

Chuck Suave is a Scottish author passionate about high-stakes, adrenaline-filled stories.

Drawing inspiration from motorsport, noir thrillers, and the psychology of redemption, he brings flawed heroes to life with raw emotion and sharp momentum. His writing blends edge-of-your-seat pacing with layered mystery, perfect for readers who like their fiction fast, gritty, and laced with suspense.

His thrillers are filled with tightly woven plots, sharp dialogue, and characters you'll remember long after the final page.

When he's not writing, he's practising Tai Chi, dodging domestic duties, or dreaming up his next high-octane plot from his home in Central Scotland

Visit Chuck: www.chucksuave.com[1]

---

1. http://www.chucksuave.com